HERGÉ

THE ADVENTURES OF TINTIN

KING OTTOKAR'S SCEPTRE

eih bennek eih blávek

D1335999

Translated by Leslie Lonsdale-Cooper
and Michael Turner

Reprinted 1991, 1992, 1993, 1994 (twice), 1995, 1996, 1997, 1998, 2001 (twice).

Printed in Belgium by Casterman Printers s.a., Tournai
ISBN 0-7497-0466-7

KING OTTOKAR'S SCEPTRE

Let's sit down on this bench for a minute.

Hello, someone has left his brief-case behind.

I can't see anybody...

Perhaps I ought to open it? The owner's name might be inside.

Here it is!... 'Hector Alembick, 24, Flyaway Road'.

That's not far. I'll take it back.

You're making a mistake, Tintin!... No good ever comes of getting mixed up in other peoples business.

FLYAWAY ROAD

Professor Alembick? Third floor, first door on the right...

24

RAT TAT TAT

Come in!

Oh, good-evening, Mrs. Piggott. Put it all on the little table, will you?

It's not Mrs. Piggott, Professor. I've brought back your brief-case.

What?...

My brief-case?

Ssh! Someone's just come to see   him...

How very kind of you to return it. I'm especially grateful, as the text of the paper I am reading to the I.S.A. Congress tonight is in there.

The I.S.A.?

I.S.A: International Sigillographical Association.

Sigi... what?

Sigillography. Do you mean you've never heard of it? It's the science concerned with the study of seals. It's extremely interesting and...A cigarette?.

No thank you: I don't smoke.

Yes, sigillography is an absorbing study. One look at my collection will convin   ce you.

?

WOOAH

Oh, good   gracious! I'm so sorry! I   have a dreadful habit of   dropping my cigarette   ends about!

This is one of the rarest items in my collection: the seal of Charlemagne. Here is the seal of Edward the Confessor, and next to it one which belonged to Gradenigo, Doge of Venice. And here's   another fine specimen: an intaglio ring   from the Saxon period

...And this is a very unusual seal, which I found quite by chance in Prague. It is the seal of Ottokar IV, King of Syldavia...

Oh?..

It is one of the few seals we know of from that country. But there must be others, and I am going to Syldavia to study the problem on the spot.

The Syldavian Ambassador, an old friend of mine, has promised to give me letters of introduction. I hope I shall be allowed to go through the historic national archives. A cigarette?...

No, thank you... And when are you leaving?

As soon as I have found a secretary. At least, rather more than a secretary; I really need someone to take care of all the details of my journey, like hotels, passports, luggage and so on.

But I see that you have become interested in sigillography too. Let me have your name and address and I will send you my booklet: 'How to become a sigillographer.'

How very kind of you...

He's going... Quick, meet him on the stairs...

Steady!..Here he comes!

'CLICK

That's a funny place to put a watch right...

Got it!... Wonderful, the way a miniature camera can be hidden in a watch...

Here!..

We'll develop the picture right away.

!?

Is it O.K.?

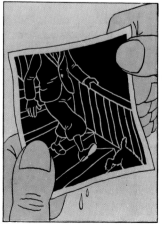

Bother! I've left my book at Professor Alembick's flat.

Anyway, we know his name is Tintin.

2nd FLOOR

?

Tintin!...Tintin!...You know that a name by itself won't do... We must have a photograph!

Well, I've had enough... I'm off... If anyone wants me, I'm at the 'KLOW'!... Goodbye!...

Goodbye!

24

This is all very mysterious... Let's follow him.

-KLOW-

SYLDAVIAN RESTAURANT

-LOW-

RESTAURANT

Well, well! 'Syldavian Restaurant'. The plot thickens!

Let's go in!

KLOW.

SYLDAVIAN

Hello?... Where's he gone?

A customer!...

Er... I'd like... something to eat...please...

Will you take a seat, sir?...

What would you like, sir?...

Er... bring me... er... a 'szlaszeck' with mushrooms ...and a glass of 'szpradj'...

But I'd like a wash first...

The cloakroom is at the end of the passage.

GENTLEMEN

...As for Professor Alembick, we'll have to wait for a day or two, until he's got the papers from the Embassy...

!

!

Ahem!

!

At the end of the passage, sir ...

GEN

I'm sorry, I misunderstood.

Did he catch me listening at the door?

...and he was listening outside the door! He's a young chap with a funny tuft of hair...There's a dog with him..

I'll bet a thousand khors it's the fellow Sporovitch tried to photograph!...

Where's Snowy got to?...

TING TING TING

My bill, please...

In a moment, sir...

What does this mean?

What, sir?... Oh, yes... Don't you know the old Syldavian custom, sir?... In res- taurants in my country there 's always a proverb or a short motto on the bill.

Oh, really?

Yes, sir. Rather nice, isn't it?... Thank you, just right... I hope you enjoyed your meal, sir? ...

Very much, thank you. Your 'szlaszeck' was excellent. How do you make it?

Ah, it's one of our specialities: the hind leg of a young dog, in Syl- davian sauce...

SNOWY!

SNOWY! SNOWY!

Ah, there you are! ...Where have you been hiding?

I hope you will come again, sir.

Ha! ha! ha! We shan't see him again in a hurry!

SERVICE

Well I'm...!

Odd! All very odd!...

HIC

JAMES

HIC

A few minutes later...

Suf... Sur... Syb... Ah, here it is! Syldavia: a State in the Balkan Peninsula. In the XIIth century Syldavia was conquered by the Bordurians

RRRRING
RRRRING
RRRRING

Hello?... Yes, it's me... Yes of course it's me... I... Who are you?... What? You'll tell me later?... Can you come and see me? What about?... Oh!... All right, I'll expect you about half past eight... Goodbye...

A man with a foreign accent, with something very important to tell me...?

HIC

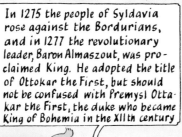

In 1275 the people of Syldavia rose against the Bordurians, and in 1277 the revolutionary leader, Baron Almaszout, was proclaimed King. He adopted the title of Ottokar the First, but should not be confused with Premysl Ottakar the First, the duke who became King of Bohemia in the XIIth century

HIC

Twenty past eight. My mysterious foreigner should soon be here.

HIC

TINTIN

RRRING

HIC

?

You have a fine way of welcoming people!... Oho! What's all this?

?

Help me to lift him on to the sofa, would you?...

Is he... dead?

But tell us what happened.

No, he's alive; his heart is beating.

What happened?... Well, about an hour ago this man rang up and asked to see me, and I agreed. At half past eight the bell rang; I opened the door and without a word the poor fellow collapsed at my feet...

Hmm!..

You said, 'without a word'... In that case, how do you know that this was the man who telephoned?...

I don't know, but it seemed likely...

And what about all this evidence of a struggle?

Evidence of a struggle, my foot! The only struggle I had was with the window, which wouldn't open! You aren't trying to say that I knocked this man out?

I didn't say that, but...

Excuse me, gentlemen...

May I ask what I am doing here?...

I rather think I should be asking you that question...

To begin with, can you describe your assailant?

My assailant?... What assailant?

Now don't try any funny business with us, my friend... Come on, what's your name?

I... let's see... It's really very odd, but I... I can't remember!...

9

Nobody... The street's quite empty..

Ah! There's a note tied to this stone..

For the last time : mind your own business !

'For the last time'... In other words, 'we have already warned you'. But when?... Why, that must have been a warning at the 'Klow'. Of course... they were Syldavians! I've got an idea!... What if I become the professor's secretary and go with him to Syldavia ?...

Next day...

Bad news!...That Tintin went to see Professor Alembick this morning and agreed to go with him to Syldavia as his secretary!... He's busy getting his passport now. If he goes with the professor our plan is bound to fail !...

You'd better leave this to me; I'll see that Tintin doesn't go!

Some hours later...

Mr. Tintin ?... He's gone out.

What's that, my boy ?

It's a parcel for Mr. Tintin.

Give me that. We'll wait for Tintin upstairs, and give him this ourselves...

But...

That's enough: we're the police!

Look, there's a letter with the parcel ... Should we open it ?...

'If you want an explanation of yesterday's events, you will find it in this parcel. A Friend.'

Excellent!... What a stroke of luck. Now we shall find something interesting...

There are two men waiting in your room; they told me they were from the police...

Oh?...Good!

I wonder what they've got to tell me...

BOOM

!?

There it goes!

BOOM

?

What have you done? What's happened?...

Er... there was a parcel for you...

... and a letter... Here: read it... We opened the parcel. We heard a 'fizz' and we just had time to throw it away, or it would have blown up in our faces!

Let's get nearer; we can mix with the crowd...

A bomb!... The cunning scoundrels!... They wanted to kill me!

!?

Quick, downstairs!... The men who did it are out there!...

Hurry! Hurry!

There they are!

It's him!

He's alone!... We'll fix him!... Let him gradually close up on us...

We're catching up!

Now we've got 'em!...

Now then, jam on the brakes ... Wham!...

!?

This time I think we've really shaken him off for good.

Where's Snowy?...And the others?...What's happened to them?

It can't be true! Surely... yes, it's them! ...Where have they come from?

You started off so suddenly that we... we couldn't keep up with you. So we commandeered this car. Shall we follow them?...

It's no good: they're too far ahead.

I'll leave you here. I must go and pack my things at once. I am going to Syldavia tomorrow.

RRRRING
RRRRING
RRRRING
RRRRING

RRRRING

Hello?...Yes... Ah, good-evening, Professor... Yes, everything is ready for our trip... Yes, I have booked seats on the Klow plane...We'll meet at the airport in the morning, at 11 o'clock...

We go via Prague, yes...Well, goodbye till tomorrow, Professor.. Yes... I... Hello?... Hello?... Hello?...

Oooooh... Help!... Help!... Aaaaaah!...

?

The professor is in danger! Quick! quick! There's not a moment to lose!...

24

I only hope I'm not too late!...

Ah! It's you, Tintin. Have you come to help me finish my packing?...

I ... I'm sorry, but I don't understand!... I thought I heard you cry out and shout for help...So I rushed straight round...

Me shouting for help?.. I'm afraid I don't know what you're talking about.

But it's extraodinary!... I can't have been dreaming! ...I quite definitely heard shouts for help...

Next morning...

It's very kind of you to come and see me off.

But of course we've come...

To be precise: of course...

Professor, may I introduce Mr. Thomson and Mr. Thompson, of the C.I.D. ... Professor Alembick, sigillographer.

How do you do?

Very well, thank you.

Oh, you've got new hats?

Yes, aren't they smart?... Pure English felt, extra-light: only £3-95. Wonderful bar-gain!

All passengers for Prague, this way please...

Well, goodbye, and bon voyage!...

And good luck in Syldavia!

Thanks.

Compression! Petrol on! Contact!

Come and look what a pretty picture these sheep make... down in that field.

Can you see them, down there?

Yes... How tiny they are: you can hardly see them...

?

How odd...

Are we landing?...

Yes: it's Frankfurt. They touch down for a few minutes.

Mr. Alembick? There's a telegram for you.

Aha!...

Here's some good news... The Syldavian government has put a special aircraft at our disposal. Look...

Sweets... Sandwiches... Chocolates... Cigarettes...

'Professor Alembick, passenger aboard aircraft No.573 OO-AGE. Frankfurt Airport. Special plane for Klow will meet you at Prague. Stop. Best wishes.' It's signed Schzlozitch, Air Minister...

I think they're calling us...

?

All passengers for Prague, please take your seats in the aircraft...

OO-AGE

It's really very odd...

Oh, well, let's forget it and look at this brochure...

SYLDAVIA
KINGDOM OF THE
BLACK PELICAN

SYLÐAVIA
THE KINGDOM OF THE BLACK PELICAN

AMONG the many enchanting places which deservedly attract foreign visitors with a love for picturesque ceremony and colourful folklore, there is one small country which, although relatively unknown, surpasses many others in interest. Isolated until modern times because of its inaccessible position, this country is now served by a regular air-line network, which brings it within the reach of all who love unspoiled beauty, the proverbial hospitality of a peasant people, and the charm of medieval customs which still survive despite the march of progress.

This is Syldavia.

Syldavia is a small country in Eastern Europe, comprising two great valleys: those of the river Vladir, and its tributary, the Moltus. The rivers meet at Klow, the capital (122,000 inhabitants). These valleys are flanked by wide plateaux covered with forests, and are surrounded by high, snow-capped mountains. In the fertile Syldavian plains are corn-lands and cattle pastures. The subsoil is rich in minerals of all kinds.

Numerous thermal and sulphur springs gush from the earth, the chief centres being at Klow (cardiac diseases) and Kragoniedin (rheumatic complaints).

The total population is estimated to be 642,000 inhabitants.

Syldavia exports wheat, mineral-water from Klow, firewood, horses and violinists.

HISTORY OF SYLDAVIA

Until the VIth century, Syldavia was inhabited by nomadic tribes of unknown origin.

Overrun by the Slavs in the VIth century, the country was conquered in the Xth century by the Turks, who drove the Slavs into the mountains and occupied the plains.

In 1127, Hveghi, leader of a Slav tribe, swooped down from the mountains at the head of a band of partisans and fell upon isolated Turkish villages, putting all who resisted him to the sword. Thus he rapidly became master of a large part of Syldavian territory.

A great battle took place in the valley of the Moltus near Zileheroum, the Turkish capital of Syldavia, between the Turkish army and Hveghi's irregulars.

Enfeebled by long inactivity and badly led by incompetent officers, the Turkish army put up little resistance and fled in disorder.

Having vanquished the Turks, Hveghi was elected king, and given the name Muskar, that is, The Brave (Muskh: 'brave' and Kar: 'king').

The capital, Zileheroum, was renamed Klow, that is, Freetown, (Kloho: 'to free', and Ow: 'town').

A typical fisherman from Dbrnouk (south coast of Syldavia)

Guard at the Royal Treasure House, Klow

◀ *Syldavian peasant on her way to market*

A view of Niedzdrow, in the Vladir valley ▶

THE BATTLE OF ZILEHEROUM

After a XVth century miniature

H.M. King Muskar XII, the present ruler of Syldavia in the uniform of Colonel of the Guards

struck him a blow on the head with the sceptre, laying him low and at the same time crying in Syldavian: '*Eih bennek, eih blavek!*', which can be said to mean: 'If you gather thistles, expect prickles'. And turning to his astonished court he said: '*Honi soit qui mal y pense!*'

Then, gazing intently at his sceptre, he addressed it in the following words: 'O Sceptre, thou hast saved my life. Be henceforward the true symbol of Syldavian Kingship. Woe to the king who loses thee, for I declare that such a man shall be unworthy to rule thereafter.'

And from that time, every year on St. Vladimir's Day each successor of Ottokar IV has made a great ceremonial tour of his capital.

He bears in his hand the historic sceptre, without which he would lose the right to rule; as he passes, the people sing the famous anthem:

> Syldavians unite!
> Praise our King's might:
> The Sceptre his right!

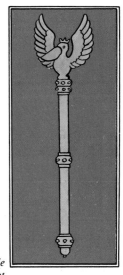

Right: The sceptre of Ottokar IV

Below: An illuminated page from 'The Memorable Deeds of Ottokar IV', a XIVth century manuscript

Muskar was a wise king who lived at peace with his neighbours, and the country prospered. He died in 1168, mourned by all his subjects.

His eldest son succeeded to the throne with the title of Muskar II.

Unlike his father, Muskar II lacked authority and was unable to keep order in his kingdom. A period of anarchy replaced one of peaceful prosperity.

In the neighbouring state of Borduria the people observed Syldavia's decline, and their king profited by this opportunity to invade the country. Borduria annexed Syldavia in 1195.

For almost a century Syldavia groaned under the foreign yoke.

In 1275 Baron Almaszout repeated the exploits of Hveghi by coming down from the hills and routing the Bordurians in less than six months.

He was proclaimed King in 1277, taking the name of Ottokar. He was, however, much less powerful than Muskar.

The barons who had helped him in the campaign against the Bordurians forced him to grant them a charter, based on the English Magna Carta signed by King John (Lackland). This marked the beginning of the feudal system in Syldavia.

Ottokar I of Syldavia should not be confused with the Ottakars (Premysls) who were Dukes, and later Kings, of Bohemia.

This period was noteworthy for the rise in power of the nobles, who fortified their castles and maintained bands of armed mercenaries, strong enough to oppose the King's forces.

But the true founder of the kingdom of Syldavia was Ottokar IV, who ascended the throne in 1370.

From the time of his accession he initiated widespread reforms. He raised a powerful army and subdued the arrogant nobles, confiscating their wealth.

He fostered the advancement of the arts, of letters, commerce and agriculture.

He united the whole nation and gave it that security, both at home and abroad, so necessary for the renewal of prosperity.

It was he who pronounced those famous words: '*Eih bennek, eih blavek*', which have become the motto of Syldavia.

The origin of this saying is as follows:

One day Baron Staszrvich, son of one of the dispossessed nobles whose lands had been forfeited to the crown, came before the sovereign and recklessly claimed the throne of Syldavia.

The King listened in silence, but when the presumptuous baron's speech ended with a demand that he deliver up his sceptre, the King rose and cried fiercely: 'Come and get it!'

Mad with rage, the young baron drew his sword, and before the retainers could intervene, fell upon the King.

The King stepped swiftly aside, and as his adversary passed him, carried forward by the impetus of his charge, Ottokar

Well, that's all very interesting, but ...

...I must be on my guard. Without his glasses this man can pick out a flock of sheep from as high up as this. He has good eyes for a short-sighted person!... And another strange thing ever since I found him packing his bags I haven't seen him smoke a single cigarette

...Unless I'm very much mistaken, I'm travelling with an impostor!... If that's so, then everything fits in...The shouts I heard on the telephone were from the real Professor Alembick. He has been kidnapped and this man has taken his place

He must be exposed! At Prague I'll pull off that false beard, and have him arrested!

Prague?... Already?

Yes, we are landing...

Now's my chance!

OH!

OUCH!

?

I...I'm sorry...I ...I missed a step ...I beg your pardon...

D-don't mention it!..

Professor Alembick?... Your special plane is wait- —ing.

It's a real beard!

But what about his glasses? ...Not that that proves anything. Plenty of people can see better at a distance than near to... As for the cigarettes, perhaps he has simply given up smoking ...

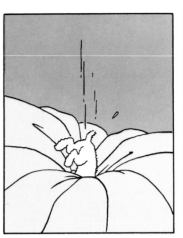

My aeroplane... BRRRR... I fell... Crash!... Into the straw...

Czestot wzryzkar nietz on vaghabontz! ...Czestot bätczer yhzer kzömmetz noh dascz politzski?...

Snowy! Snowy!

Wooah! Wooah!

Kzommet micz omhz, noh dascz politzski!

Come with you to the police?... With pleasurski! ...I've got a complaint to make!

ПОЛИЦКИ

Captain, what I have to say is of the utmost importance... May I speak to you in private?...

Er... Yes... Leave us alone...

First, may I ask you a question?... I read in a brochure about Syldavia that if your King loses his sceptre he will be forced to abdicate. Is that true?...

As a matter of fact it is... But how does this concern you?

I'll tell you. I am certain there's a conspiracy against King Muskar XII, and that certain people will try to steal the sceptre from him!

What's that you say?... What makes you imagine such a thing?

I'll explain... But first, are you sure we are not overheard?

Definitely not. Go on...

This must be serious. They've been in there nearly an hour...

АДВИЧА

You have just rendered a great service to my country: I thank you. I will telegraph at once to Klow and have Professor Alembick arrested. I'm sure I can rely on you for absolute secrecy..

Of course... But I must be on my way... Can I hire a car?

There isn't a single car in the village. But tomorrow is market-day in Klow. You can go with a peasant who is leaving here today. But you won't arrive there until morning...

Too bad, but I have no choice. I'll go with the peasant

Hello?... Yes, this is Klow 3324... Yes, Central Committee... Trovik speaking...Oh it's you Wizskitotz...What?... Tintin?...But that's impossible: the pilot has just told me... What?...Into some straw!...Szplug! He must be prevented from reaching Klow at all costs!... Do it how you like... Yes, ring up Sirov...

Hello?...Yes, this is Sirov... Hello Wizskitotz...Yes...A young boy, on the road to Klow... In a peasant's cart... Good, we'll be waiting in the forest...Yes, we'll leave at once... Goodbye!...

Look out!... Here they come!...

Hands up!...

?

Where's the young foreigner you are taking to Klow?...

Th-th- the young f-f-f-foreign -er...

That's enough!... We know he's with you!... Search the cart, Zlop!

Th-th-the f-f-foreign ...er who..who w-w-w

Was w-w-w-with m-m -me?...

What makes you stutter like that?... Fear?...

N-n-no! ...It...it...it... it's b-b-be-because...I...I... I t-t-talk...talk...talk...

Sirov! There's no one there!

Szplug! Where can he be?... Come on, are you going to talk?...

I...I...w-was g-g-going t-t-to t-tell y-y-you, b-b-bbut y-yyou in-in-inter-inter-interrupted m-m-me!... He st-st-stopped at... at...at... th-th-the Co-co-co-

Cocoa!...Cocoa!...What cocoa?.. Have you been drinking?...

The Co-Co-Coach-Coachman's Rest, an-an-and...

Why didn't you say so sooner? ...

Quiet!...I can hear a car!

An-an-and he...he...he... g-g-g-

If you say one word, or make one move...just remember our rifles are trained on you!...

L-l-l-listen ...l...l...I'm I'm...

It's gone... We can go back...

I...I'm t-t-try-trying to t-t-tell...yy-yy-yyou...th-th-the y-y-young f-f-for-foreigner w-w-

Szplitz on Szplug! Where is he?...

W-w-was in...in...in th-th-that c-c-car w-w-w-which j-j-just papa-papa-passed!...

27

Yes, I am singing tonight at the Winter Garden in Klow... Would you like to hear me now?...

I'd love to.

Ah, ♪ my beauty ♪ past compare: these jewels ♫ bright I wear!...

Was I ever Margar-i-i-ta?

It's lucky the windows are strong!

Hello?... Yes, this is Wizskitotz... Ah, it's you Sirov... Well?... What?... Szplug! ...So it's not your fault?... Perhaps you think it's mine, eh?... What?... If he hadn't stuttered so?... If!... If!... You can get round anything with 'if'... I'll telephone to the Chief of Police at Zlip... Yes, he's one of us... He'll stop him on the road.

Well, how did you like that?...

V-very much indeed!...

In that case, just to please you I'll sing something else!

!!

Where is the boy who is travelling with you?...

He got out earlier on. He'd forgotten something at the Coachman's Rest, so he went back...

I would have given any excuse to escape!

Meanwhile, in Klow...

So, you wish to have access to the Treasure House to examine the national archives?... I won't conceal from you that this is a privilege rarely accorded to a foreigner, but since our ambassador has vouched for you, I think His Majesty will look favourably upon your request

 That's him... We'll ask for his papers...

 Your papers are not in order! ... Come with us to the police station!

 Quite correct: your papers are not in order! ... I shall have to keep you here until I receive instructions

But Captain, there must be some mistake!... My passport was stamped before I left and...

 I am sorry, but I cannot allow you to proceed. Take him away!

 Captain!... You must listen!... I have something important to tell you!... I...

 Hello?... Wizskitotz?... This is Szplodj... I've got our fine bird!...Yes, we simply picked him up... Now what do you want us to do with him?... Yes...Yes... He obviously mustn't get to Klow... I'll think it over...That's it, ring up in the morning...Goodbye...

 While I cool my heels here, goodness knows what's going on in Klow...

 Aaaouaaah!...It's getting dark... I'd better try and get some sleep, as there's nothing else to do...

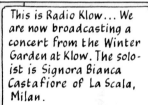

 This is Radio Klow... We are now broadcasting a concert from the Winter Garden at Klow. The soloist is Signora Bianca Castafiore of La Scala, Milan.

 ♪♪✦✶ ♪♪ # ✶ ♪ ✦ ♪

 Ah, my beauty ♪ past compare; these jewels bright I wear! ♪♪ Was I ever Margarita?

 Is it I? ♪ Come reply! ♪ Mirror, mirror tell me truly! ♪♪ ♩.

Next day...

This document bearing the royal signature will admit you to the Treasure Chamber. Lieutenant Kromir will escort you there...

The regalia is housed in the keep of Kropow Castle. A special guard is mounted over it.

In the name of the King!

Professor, please come with me.

The regalia seems well guarded!

It is! The man who is clever enough to steal it hasn't been born!

There is His Majesty's regalia, Professor!...

And this is the Muniments Room, which adjoins the Treasure Chamber. You must forgive me, but two guards will remain with you for as long as you are here. The doors will also be locked from the outside. Those are the orders. I hope you will not be offended.

Not in the least...

Meanwhile...

You are to take this young man to Klow. But be careful!... He is a dangerous ruffian who has been meddling in State secrets... In fact, I've been given to understand, on high authority, that it'd be a good thing if he never arrived in Klow

These are your orders... You, as the driver, will stage a breakdown. You will get out to look at the engine, and the others will follow... The prisoner will then try to escape and... You understand me?

Yes, sir!... But what if he doesn't try to get away?

Don't worry!... He will!...

I wonder who can have sent me this?... A friend? ... What friend?...

BEWARE!
YOU ARE GOING TO BE TAKEN TO KLOW TO BE SHOT! YOU MUST TRY TO ESCAPE. ON THE JOURNEY, PRETEND TO BE ASLEEP. THE DRIVER, WHO IS A FRIEND, WILL STAGE A BREAKDOWN AND CALL THE OTHER GUARDS AWAY. THAT WILL BE THE MOMENT FOR YOU TO MAKE YOUR ESCAPE.

A FRIEND

We'd better get rid of this, in case I'm searched.

Here, Snowy, swallow this paper pellet for me...

Hurry up now, Snowy, I think someone is coming for us...

I suppose you think it's easy?

He fell down there ... Somewhere behind those rocks...

They're coming!...

Careful! About here...

Szplug! Where is he? We've simply got to find him...The captain will never forgive us if we let him get away, after he'd planned that trap...

Come on, let's have another look. He can't be far away...

Whew!... They've passed us...

Now, off we go to Klow!...

I must watch my step!... I see that no one can be trusted!... I must warn the King himself.

Meanwhile in Klow...

I wonder if I might be permitted to photograph some of the documents?

As a rule that is not allowed, but His Majesty might consent...

Ah! Here's the main road again.

Golly, I'm hungry...

You have His Majesty's permission to photograph the documents. But the pictures may only be taken by the official Court Photographer, Herr Czarlitz. Here is the order which authorises him to go with you into the castle...

Klow at last!...

When are we going to eat?

Which way to the palace, please?

Follow this street to Ottokar Square, then turn left...

DANGER HIGH VOLTAGE

What a downpour! We'll shelter until this is over...

Is this a restaurant?

It's stopping now...

Come on Snowy!... We must hurry to warn the King of the danger he's in...

Hurry up, Snowy! Hey, where is Snowy?

Snowy!... Snowy!... Snowy! ..

They have wonderful bones in this country, Tintin!...

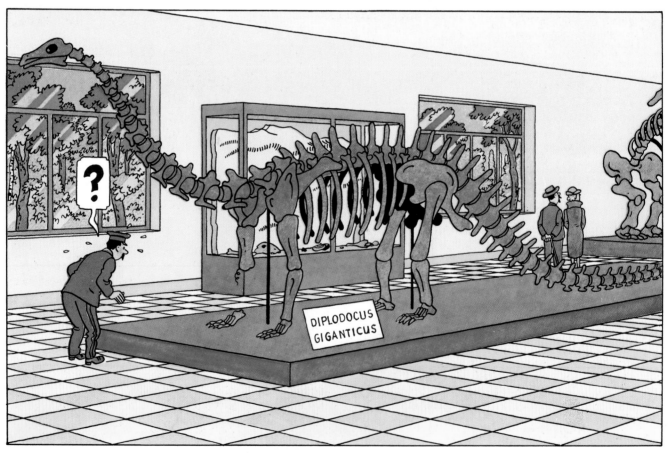
DIPLODOCUS GIGANTICUS

You take that bone back where you found it, at once! You understand...And be quick!...

Ah! There's the palace!

Could His Majesty grant me an audience?... I have most important and urgent business...

Please wait here: I will see if His Majesty's aide-de-camp will see you. Whom shall I announce?...

Tintin.

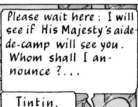

Mr. Tintin?... On important business?... All right, show him in.

Certainly, Signora... Yes... yes ... tonight, at half-past eight ... His Majesty will be delighted ...Your servant, Signora...

Meanwhile...

So that's all arranged, Herr Czarlitz... I will come and fetch you in the morning at about nine, and we will go to Kropow Castle together...

Very good, Professor.

So you want an audience with His Majesty?... May I ask why?...

Er...I... you must excuse me, but... it is highly confidential....

Sir, I am His Majesty's aide-de-camp!...I venture to say that my sovereign places complete trust in me!

I do not doubt it, Colonel!...But the news I have to communicate to the King is so serious that it is for his ears alone.

Very well, I will not insist...Will you come back tonight, at about half past eight? I will try and arrange for His Majesty to allow you a few minutes, before his reception at the palace...

Thank you very much.

Now for a meal, Snowy!

Hello?...Yes, this is the Central Committee. Ah, it's you, Boris. What's the latest news? ...Yes...What?...Tintin?...Are you sure? But the Chief of Police at Zlip has just sworn that... Yes...Terribly important information

But he didn't say what it was?.. Good!...Aha!...He'll be back tonight at eight-thirty?...That's fine, it gives us time...Listen, he must not speak to the King... Definitely not!...This is what we'll do: listen...

That evening...

The King is willing to grant you a short interview. Please go with the Captain of the Guard and he will take you to the Audience Chamber. His Majesty will see you there.

Thank you.

Ssh!...Here they come...

Wooah! Wooah!

?

That mongrel has given us away!...Come on!..

An ambush!...

Got you, my friend. Don't try to resist!...

!

Traitor!...

BONK

Thanks Snowy

That's knocked out all four! Fine! Now, let's try and see the King..

He should be in here...

?

Next morning..

More time wasted!... And I'm sure the conspirators won't be wasting theirs! ...

CLINK
CLINK
CLINK

You are being transferred to the State Prison to await trial. Come with us. The police van is outside...

Hello, this is St. Vladimir's Hospital...An accident?... ....Casualties? In Moltus Street? ...All right, I'll send an ambulance

This one still hasn't come round...

Yes, definitely suffering from concussion...

We'd better go back for the others...

A very useful thing, concussion ... Come on, Snowy! Now or never ...

Aha! That's done the trick!... Now back to the palace!

I must see the King at all costs.

This time nothing is going to stop me speaking to him!...

You aren't hurt, I hope?

No, thank you. I'm all right...Great snakes!..The King!

Take care, Sire!...This is the young anarchist who tri—ed...

?

Don't shoot, Sir!...Please listen!...I am not an anarchist. I wanted to warn you...Even at this moment those scoundrels may be trying to steal your sceptre!

What do you mean?

It's the truth, Sir. I am certain that Professor Alembick is an impostor. Coming to Syldavia to study the archives was only a blind. He and his accomplices plan to steal King Ottokar's sceptre, and so force you to give up your throne!

By Vladimir! Can it be?

Meanwhile...

And this man is in with them, Sir...That is why he tried to stop me speaking to you!...

It's a lie, Sire!

He's in the plot too?

He is lying, Sire, and I will...

You will return to the palace at once and await my orders!...I myself will go to Kropow Castle with this young man and prove for myself the truth of his allegations !...

We must hurry, Sir...I'm sure there's not a moment to lose...

That's that...May we now go into the Treasure Chamber, and photograph the crown and sceptre?...

Certainly.

The light is not very good. We'll have to use a flash-bulb...

We're nearly there... Those are the towers of Kropow Castle... the sceptre is in the keep, that square tower in the centre... I only hope we're not too late!...

The King!...

Everything seems quite normal... We are in time!

I hope so, Sir...

Where is Professor Alembick?

In the Treasure Chamber, Sire, with the Governor of the Castle and Herr Czarlitz..

Open up! In the name of the King!

No answer! Quick, bring me the other keys!

Could it really be possible?

Let us hope not, Sir... Ah! Here is the guard with the keys.

So, Lord Chamberlain, the sceptre has not been recovered yet?...

Alas no, Sire...But I have secured the services of two detectives of international repute.. expect them any minute now...

THUD

Ah, I think I know who they are.

What's going on?... Go and see.

?

Er...We are the detectives who...Hm...We ...we slipped...and ...

Yes. and we fell down...

Sire, may I present Mr. Thomson and Mr. Thompson, certified detectives...

Welcome to Syldavia, gentlemen...

Majesty, your sire is very good...Good Majesty...no, I mean..

To be precise...it's a majesty, Your Pleasure...

We thank you for answering our call so promptly, and for placing your experience at the service of the Crown...This is Mr. Tintin, who will give you all the details of this business..

Tintin! Well I never!

This is the position...Someone has stolen the King's sceptre!...When His Majesty and I entered the Treasure Chamber we found the Governor of the Castle, two of his men, the photographer Czarlitz, and Professor Alembick, whom you know. All of them were in a coma, and none of the five came to until this morning...

Have they been questioned?...

Yes, and their statements agree on all points. Herr Czarlitz decided to use a flash-bulb. After the flash the room filled with thick smoke. They began to choke, and then passed out...

Good. But...hm...did anyone think of searching these people?...

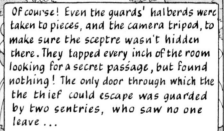

Of course! Even the guards' halberds were taken to pieces, and the camera tripod, to make sure the sceptre wasn't hidden there. They tapped every inch of the room looking for a secret passage, but found nothing! The only door through which the thief could escape was guarded by two sentries, who saw no one leave...

Your Majesty, this is all childishly simple!... With your permission we will go to Kropow Castle and demonstrate how your sceptre was stolen...

Very well, we'll go!...

Goodness, they're smarter than I thought!

Be careful: the marble is very slippery ...

This is the Treasure Chamber. The sceptre was here...

As we said, Your Majesty: the whole thing is childishly simple!

This is what happened. One of the five people present was in the plot. He collapsed when the smoke was released, but took care to hold a handkerchief to his nose. When he was sure the others had been put to sleep he got up, opened the glass case, seized the sceptre, opened the window and dropped the sceptre into the courtyard. There an accomplice collected it, took it away, and that was that!

Impossible, gentlemen! The courtyard is guarded. No one goes there but the sentries; and the sentries are above suspicion... They are men of absolute trust who would die rather than betray their King!

As a matter of fact the guard patrolling this side of the tower did hear a window open and shut. But he did not notice anything unusual...

Exactly!... Because the thief must have thrown the sceptre over the ramparts surrounding the castle!... An accomplice waited there, picked it up, and made off.

However, you shall see... Could you get me something the same size as the sceptre?...

Certainly...

But look! It is at least a hundred yards from this window to the ramparts! ...And there are bars...

What do they matter?... It just needs a good aim...

There... Will this do?...

Perfectly

Now I'll show you...

? BONG

Clumsy oaf!... Let me show you the right way to do it!...

Watch carefully!...

BONG ?

You can see for yourselves that the sceptre didn't leave this room like that!...

Yes...Yes...maybe. Anyway, we'd like to question Alembick and Czarlitz...

Sire!... Sire!... Ah, at last I've found you...

?

45

What happened ?... Quick, tell us!...

The camera !... Look at the camera !...

A spring ?...

Yes, this spring came out. It hit me in the face and knocked me out !...

It's amazing !... How did you discover that?

By walking past a toy-shop! ...I saw a little spring gun; it gave me the idea that perhaps the camera was faked up to hide a spring capable of throwing the sceptre beyond the castle ramparts! And my guess was right!...

Watch!... There's the spring back in place... I insert into the tube this stick used by the two detectives...

I place the camera by the window, the forked end of our makeshift sceptre through the bars...

I click the shutter, and ... Whoops!

It's fallen in the wood, beyond the river!... I'm going to have a look round over there.

You will find a boat down by the bank...

?

If that fool Czarlitz had aimed at the clump of birch trees by the river bank as we agreed, we'd have found the sceptre long ago...

!

So they haven't found it yet! ...There's not a moment to lose!...I must get back, and have this wood surrounded.

?

HOORAY!...

Hooray! I've found it!

!

Now, I must give the others the slip...

Crumbs! They've got me!

Yes, got you allright!

The sceptre, Snowy!... Save the sceptre!...

How did you know I was here?

When we went back to the castle they told us you had crossed the river...

There's the King... They told him, too. He went round by the bridge while we crossed in a boat...

Well, what has happened?...

Those gangsters have got away in a car, with the sceptre!... If you will lend us your car, Sir, we three will try and catch them...

They haven't got much of a start on us... We'll soon catch them up.

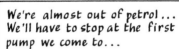

We're almost out of petrol... We'll have to stop at the first pump we come to...

Ah! There's one...

Five gallons!... And make it snappy!...

Another twenty miles to the frontier... Good!... In half an hour we shall be clear of Syldavia, and the sceptre will be safe!

The King's car!... They're after us!

We certainly caught them on the hop!... They've taken to the mountains!

They hadn't even time to get back into their car...

We must hurry!... They musn't get away!

They're still following us...

We must stop this! ... We'll fool them! ...

Come on!... We'll get them!...

BANG

Take cover everybody... They are shooting at us!

BANG

Where have Thomson and Thompson got to?... I can't see them anywhere.

BANG

CRACK

There must be some way of catching them...

Follow me, Snowy, and don't show yourself!... We'll sneak round behind them.

Hello, where's the third one?...

Not a sign of life...

Perhaps we hit him... Look! There are the other two...

Hands up!

Now, I see!... You blocked our way while your pal got away with the sceptre!...

Quick! You look after these thugs!... I'm going on...

Szplug! I can't understand it. ... He's still on my tail!...

It's getting dark... We can't keep this up much longer.

We can't go on now... We'll have to spend the night here!...

We can only wait until it's light...

Next day, at dawn...

Off we go Snowy!... We simply must recover the sceptre!

We'll walk fast: That will warm us up...

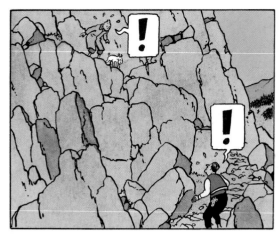

One day you'll break your neck with all those acrobatics!...

Let's search him... Ah! Here's his wallet...

?

Z.Z.R.K.   1239
SECRET   To Section Commanders, Shock Troops
SUBJECT: Seizure of Power
I wish to draw your attention to the order in which the operations for seizure of power in Syldavia will take place.
On the eve of St. Vladimir's Day, agents in our propaganda units will foment incidents, and arrange for Bordurian nationals to be beaten up.
On St. Vladimir's Day, at 12 o'clock (H-hour), shock troops will seize Radio Klow, the airfield, the gas works and power station, the banks, the general post office, the Royal Palace, Kropow Castle, etc...
In due course each section commander will receive precise orders concerning his particular mission.
I salute you!
(signed)
Müsstler.

Z.Z.R.K.   1240
SECRET   To Section Commanders, Shock Troops
SUBJECT: Seizure of Power
I wish to remind you that I shall broadcast a call to arms when Radio Klow is in our hands.
Motorized Bordurian troops will then cross into Syldavian territory, to free our native land from the tyranny of King Muskar XII.
Allowing for the feeble resistance they may meet with from a few fanatical royalist partisans and certain subversive sections of the populace, the Bordurian troops will arrive in Klow at about 5.0 p.m.
I call upon all members of Z.Z.R.K. to defend until then, with the last drop of their blood, the positions they will have occupied at midday.
I salute you!
(signed)
Müsstler.

There's no time to lose! We must get back to Klow as fast as we can...

Not on foot I hope?

What's the matter with me?

Oh, I know... I haven't eaten anything since yesterday! If only I had some food!

There's a house over there... But it's across the frontier. Can't be helped... I'm too hungry!

A Bordurian frontier post!...

Crumbs! He's come to... I'm cut off!

BANG

WOOF WOOF

He's a dangerous Syldavian spy!... We must capture him!...

Look out! He may be hiding in that house ...

No, he's gone... Come on!

What's the matter with him?

SNIFF

What's he sniffing at?...

SNIFF
SNIFF
SNIFF

Pep...Tchoo!... It's pepper...Aaaa ...tchoo!

Little devil! He's scattered pepper to put the dog off the scent!

Hello!... Searchlights!

They've picked us up!... I hope they...

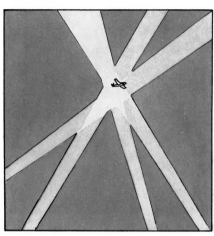

Crumbs!...They're firing... at me!

Got him!... Look, he's on fire...

Ah, a signpost!... That's a stroke of luck!

ISTOW 19½ miles
KLOW 15¾ miles

Sixteen miles: that's five hours' walk!...

A mere trifle!

A farm!... Stables!... If only I could borrow a horse...

That's a splendid idea!

Aha, here's a horse!... Whoa there!... Good, here's a saddle too... Whoa now! Gently does it...

On the whole I think we'd better go on foot.

Why not?... A little walk will do us good.

That night...

Things are grave, Sire!... the people are suspicious: there are rumours that the sceptre is missing. Furthermore...

..Bordurian shops were looted again yesterday. These incidents are of course the work of agitators in the pay of a foreign power, but we are faced with a dangerous situation. And if Your Majesty appears before the crowds without the sceptre, I fear...

Rest assured, Prime Minister, there will be no bloodshed. I will abdica te.

No, Sir, you will not abdicate...

!

TINTIN!

?

Your Majesty, I have your sceptre with me now!

Saved!

Here it is!... I... Great snakes! I've lost it on the way!

Lucky I saw the sceptre fall out of his pocket!

!

???

Saved!... I am saved!... How happy this makes me!

Saved for the moment only, Sir. I have discovered something else...

I found these on the ruffians I went after.

'Seizure of power'!... And it's signed Müsstler! ...Müsstler, the leader of the Iron Guard!

Not a moment to lose! Arrest Müsstler and his associates at once!

Yes, Sire!...

General, the review of the army will not take place tomorrow as arranged. By 8 a.m., crack regiments will occupy defensive positions along the frontier. And take over all the strategic points which the rebels plan to attack...

Very good, Sire!

Some hours later...

COCKADOODLEDOO

BOOM

BOOM

Guns!...

Come in!

RAT
TAT
TAT

Oh, it's you!...What is all that firing for?

That?...

They are firing a salute for St. Vladimir's Day... Hurry up and dress, or we shall miss the procession.

And so the royal carriage leaves the palace... the King, smiling, bare-headed, is holding the Sceptre of Ottokar in his hand... A great roar of welcome greets His Majesty, a roar which fades only when the strains of our national anthem swell from a thousand voices...

And now the King is once more in his palace. Time and again the delirious crowds have called His Majesty back on to the balcony to receive their tumultuous acclaim. But now he is seated here in the Throne Room, where an investiture is taking place...

My Lords, Ladies and Gentlemen. Never in our long history has the Order of the Golden Pelican been conferred upon a foreigner. But today with the full agreement of Our ministers, We bestow this high distinction upon Mr. Tintin, to express Our gratitude for the great services he has rendered to Our country..

Tintin, Knight of the Order of the Golden Pelican...

Hurrah!... Hurrah!...

Some days later...

MINISTRY OF THE INTERIOR

OFFICE OF THE MINISTER

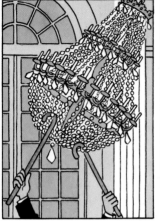

I expect you will like to hear the result of our enquiries. You already know that Müsstler, leader of the Iron Guard, has been arrested with most of his followers. Calling themselves the Iron Guard they were in fact the Z.Z.R.K., the Zyldav Zentral Revolutzionär Komitzät, whose aims were the deposition of our King, and the annexation of our country by Borduria...

Professor Alembick was also arrested at Müsstler's home where he hid after the theft of the sceptre. This little book was found on him...

Stassanov, Igor. Ambassador. A very close friend. Met him in Belgrade in 1913 at a sigillographical congress. Gave me a letter of introduction to study national archives in Klow. He

Kavarovitch Syldavian Secret Agent. Keeps an eye on Syldavian organisations abroad. Pretends to be an artist. Seems to suspect something of him! LIQUIDATE

I know him. He's the man who collapsed in my room! But look!.. That's me!...

Tintin. Reporter. Brought back my briefcase. Showed him my collection of seals. Mentioned my visit to Zyldavia. Said a secretary Promised to send him my book on DON'T TRUST HIM!

It's incredible!... But what was this note book for?...

So that they would know everyone who went to see the real Professor Alembick... Here is another photograph found at Müsstler's house which is the key to the puzzle...

Twins!... I might have guessed it!... But what happened to the real professor?...

Well, I've just read the London newspapers. Listen: 'During a search carried out yesterday in a house occupied by Syldavian nationals, the police found Professor Alembick, the scholar. He had been imprisoned in a cellar for some weeks. He said he had been kidnapped on the eve of his departure for Syldavia, and his passport was taken...'

Now I see it all! First the shouts on the telephone; then the professor not wearing his glasses, and not smoking any more... It explains everything.

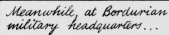

Meanwhile, at Bordurian military headquarters...

...to prove our peaceful intentions, despite the inexplicable attitude of the Syldavians, I have ordered our troops to withdraw fifteen miles from the frontier...

Next day...

In private audience this morning the King received Mr. Tintin, Mr. Thomson and Mr. Thompson, who paid their respects before leaving Syldavia. Afterwards the party left by road for Douma, where they embarked in a flying-boat of the regular Douma-Southampton service...

RADIO KLOW SZCHT-SILENCE

Some hours later...

Ten past six. We're there...

Goodness, what on earth's happening?..

We're falling into the sea...

We aren't FALLING; we're landing! This is a flying-boat, remember!

? ?

How absurd!... I had completely forgotten!

Me too!... That was a good joke!

SY·AMO

Isn't it amazing how absent-minded one can be!

Quite absurd!

I can still hear you shouting: 'We're falling into the sea'!

Ha Ha! Ha Ha! Ha Ha!

SY·AMO

AMO

HERGÉ

eih bennek · eih blavek